For Sander, Mikkel, Kian, Eliah and Lucy.

Title: Timothy Mean and the Time Machine
Author: William AE Ford.
Website: www.williamaeford.com

© William A E Ford 2019

First published 2019

ISBN: 9781730758072

Illustrated by Marcelo Simonetti
www.marcelosimonetti.com

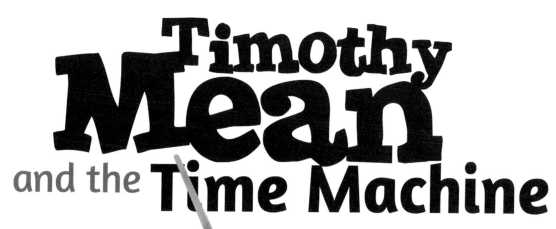

Timothy Mean
and the Time Machine

William A.E. Ford

Illustrated by
Marcelo Simonetti

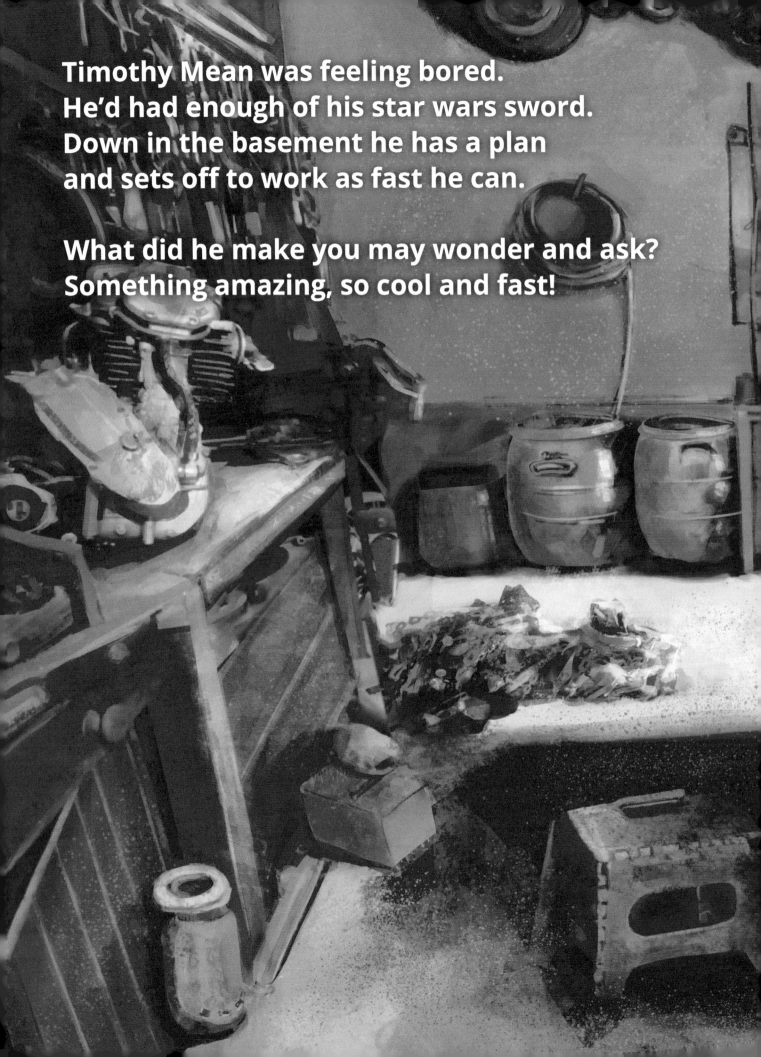

Timothy Mean was feeling bored.
He'd had enough of his star wars sword.
Down in the basement he has a plan
and sets off to work as fast he can.

What did he make you may wonder and ask?
Something amazing, so cool and fast!

From cardboard boxes, and sticky glue
it smoked and gurgled and bubbled too.
A big red GO button that he could press
to travel through time. It was the best!

Timothy Mean built a time machine.
An amazing thing that had to be seen.

It's Monday. Hip hip hooray!
Where shall we travel in time today?
Push the button, off we go.
Where are we going? Nobody knows.

To a Viking ship on a sea so stormy.
Helmets and axes in all their glory.
They sailed the sea to lands untold
and stole all the food and drink and gold.
The leader's name was Tor the Weird
An enormous man with a big black beard.
When Tor was sleeping late at night,
Timothy gave him the utmost fright.
He snipped and cut his facial hair
so it looked just like a teddy bear.
What a giggle - oh so much fun.
Back off home to tell dad and mum.

It's Tuesday. Hip hip hooray! Where shall we travel in time today?
Push the button, off we go. Where are we going? Nobody knows.

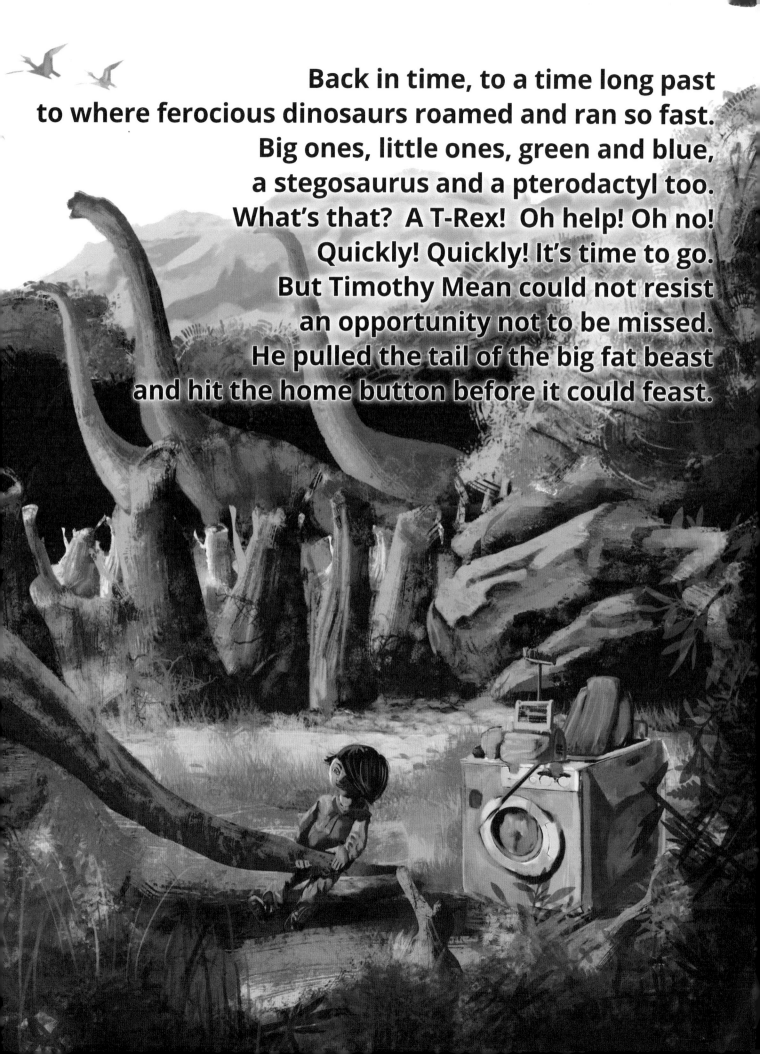

Back in time, to a time long past
to where ferocious dinosaurs roamed and ran so fast.
Big ones, little ones, green and blue,
a stegosaurus and a pterodactyl too.
What's that? A T-Rex! Oh help! Oh no!
Quickly! Quickly! It's time to go.
But Timothy Mean could not resist
an opportunity not to be missed.
He pulled the tail of the big fat beast
and hit the home button before it could feast.

It's Wednesday. Hip hip hooray! Where shall we travel in time today?
Push the button, off we go. Where are we going? Nobody knows.

Back in time to when mummy & daddy were small
In fact they both were still at school.
He dropped a water bomb on daddy's head
And put yucky things on mummy's bread.
Daddy cried and said boo-hoo,
while Timothy blew raspberries at the teacher too.
Home we go, the day gets better.
Let's hope mum and dad don't remember!

It's Thursday. Hip hip hooray! Where shall we
travel in time today?
Push the button, off we go. Where are we going?
Nobody knows.

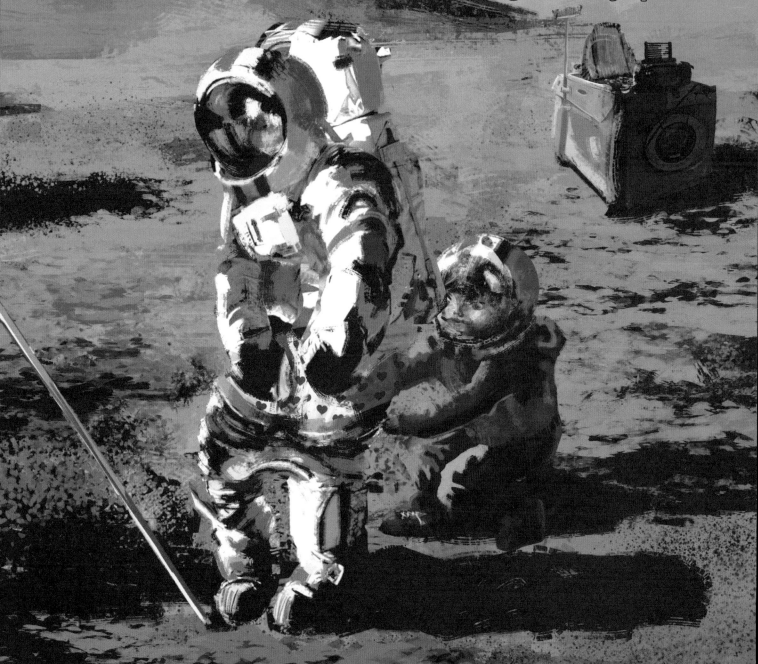

Oh what fun to go back in time,
This time to 1969
when the first man went up to the moon
in a rocket ship, zoom-zoom zoom-zoom.
Neil Armstrong was the astronaut's name.
What an opportunity to play a game!
He pulled down his trousers just before
he planted his flag, which the whole world saw.
What a very naughty trick!
Better get home again very quick.

It's Friday. Hip hip hooray!
Where shall we travel in time today?
Push the button, off we go.
Where are we going? Nobody knows.

To a castle with turrets high
and a dragon flying up in the sky.
With knights and swords, and a king and queen,
Oh what fun for Timothy Mean.
He hopped upon the dragon's wing
and flew him down to meet the king.
Past the guards and all the knights
who tried in vain to stop his flight.
The king cried "mummy" and hid under the bed,
while Timothy stroked the nice dragon's head.
He'd had his fun. It was time to go.
What a naughty so and so.

It's Saturday. Hip hip hooray!
Where shall we travel in time today?
Push the button, off we go.
Where are we going? Nobody knows.

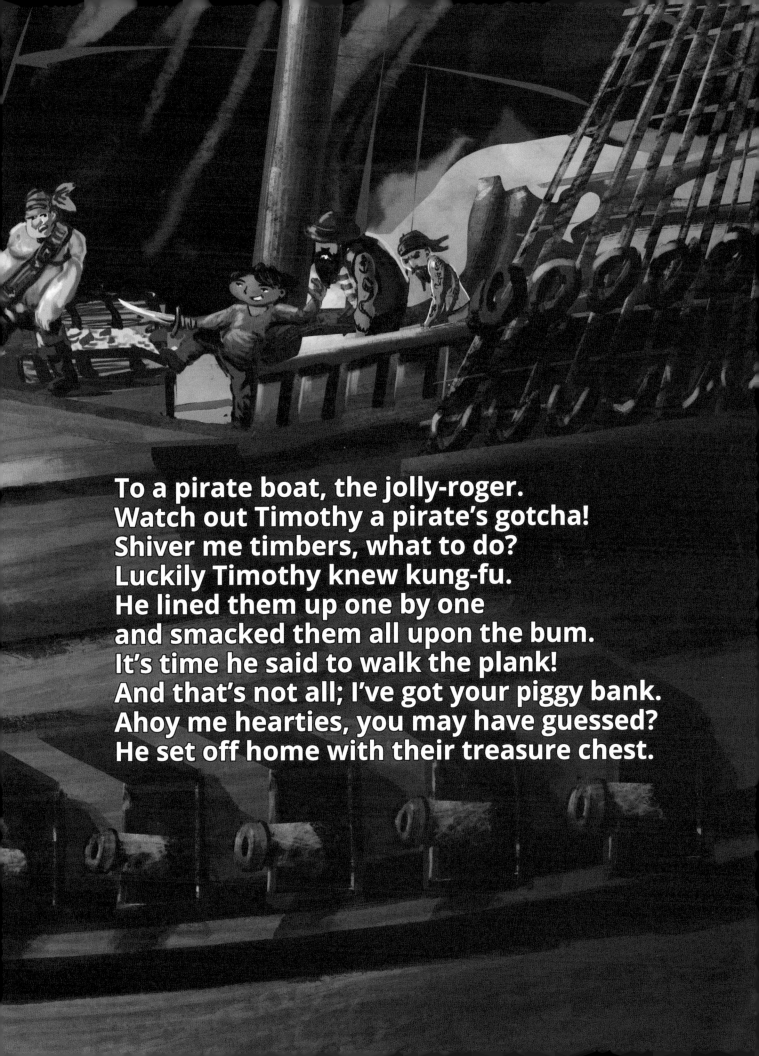

To a pirate boat, the jolly-roger.
Watch out Timothy a pirate's gotcha!
Shiver me timbers, what to do?
Luckily Timothy knew kung-fu.
He lined them up one by one
and smacked them all upon the bum.
It's time he said to walk the plank!
And that's not all; I've got your piggy bank.
Ahoy me hearties, you may have guessed?
He set off home with their treasure chest.

It's Sunday. Hip hip hooray!
Where shall we travel in time today?
Push the button, off we go.
Where are we going? Nobody knows.

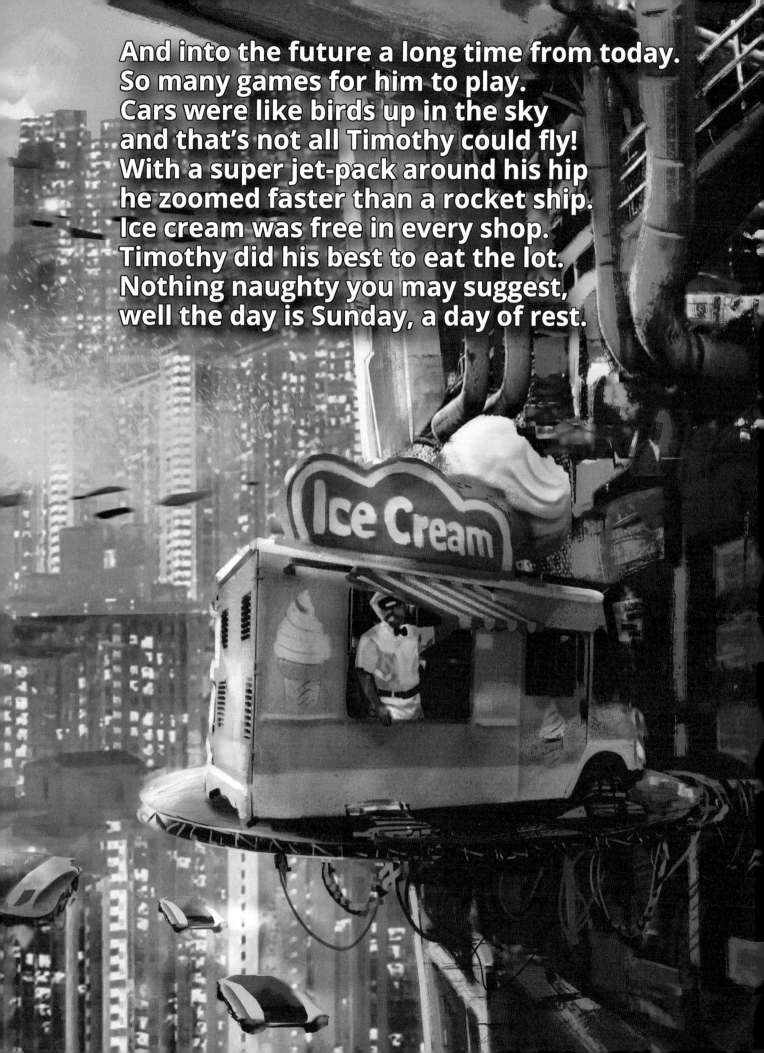

And into the future a long time from today.
So many games for him to play.
Cars were like birds up in the sky
and that's not all Timothy could fly!
With a super jet-pack around his hip
he zoomed faster than a rocket ship.
Ice cream was free in every shop.
Timothy did his best to eat the lot.
Nothing naughty you may suggest,
well the day is Sunday, a day of rest.

Timothy found the central switch
and turned them all off without a glitch.
The kids were joyous, school was closed all week.
Timothy Mean, what a sneak.

What an adventure, so much fun he had.
What a playful mind, said mum and dad.

Printed in Great Britain
by Amazon